TAIL TALKS

BY DEBORAH A. HESSELBEIN, M.A.
ILLUSTRATED BY NORMA L. CLAYCOMB

First published by Dog Ear Publishing
4010 W. 86th Street, Ste H
Indianapolis, IN 46268
www.dogearpublishing.net

ISBN: 978-159858-560-5

This book is printed on acid-free paper.
This book is a work of Fiction. Places, events, and situations in this book are purely
Fictional and any resemblance to actual persons, living or dead, is coincidental.

Printed in the United States of America

DEDICATION

This story is dedicated to
Hannah, Jennifer, Lisa, Kimmie, and Rocio, my precious "daughters",
and their children.

And to all the children found within the Human Services System and those amazing human service and criminal justice professionals, who desire to serve children during such a stressful and confusing time in their young lives. It is dedicated to those parents, who strive to work through their struggles so that they can be reunited with their children, and to those who open their hearts and homes to adopt our most vulnerable citizens.

IN GRATITUDE

I would like to express my heartfelt thanks to the following individuals who have helped to make this book a reality:

My mother and advisory board chairwoman of DestinyCubed, Doris Hesselbein, for her constant support and love. Norma Claycomb, the reluctant illustrator and incredible role model for my entire life. Donna Craft, my best friend and sister, who has faithfully supported all my endeavors with confidence in my abilities and a smile on her face most of the time. Marile Robinson, who has always known this book was possible.

My very own Olivia, who counsels, guides, and teaches me about human nature, the powerful psychology of the mind, and the ability to heal with words.

Connie Van Guilder, my chief editor who read this story so many times that the characters are forever imbedded in her mind, taking time to gently critique my work, providing an understandable tale. Dale Harrington, Anat and Michael Wolin for the final proofs read with fresh eyes, and Leor Wolin, who guided the technology of this project with creativity and expertise.

Miles, Ray, Matt, and Alan, my publishers at DogEar Publishing Company, who were committed to producing a book worthy of the young and older readers who would be touched by their combined quality of excellence in their product.

Annika, Katie, Will, and Diane Hesselbein, who listened with ears of children and read with a heart of a mother to provide feedback regarding the impact of this unique animal story on the hearts of children.

And most of all, to the One who created forest animals, and has provided mankind with the ability to create an imaginary world that can take those who are afraid, lonely, confused, lost, and hopeless into a realm of fiction that may provide comfort and hope while they gain their strength to continue life's incredible journey.

I am so grateful and love each of you!

CHAPTER I

Crash, bang, splat!

Once upon a time, not far from here, near the quiet, old Lake Haven Lodge, built up against a beautiful forest...

"Please Rochelle, you must be much quieter or they will hear you Dear!"

"I can climb up here Mama and get the lid off."

Clang, bang, crash, "yeowwwwww, Mama, help!" ... truck lights beamed bright on the eyes of the thief. Mama froze in the light, startled by the commotion of dogs barking, porch lights going on, and humans rushing toward her. "Run, Rochelle, run and keep running, Child. Run, Precious, run!"

The tiny raccoon raced for the forest trees, afraid to stop, but turned to look back. "Mama!" She cried out, as only a baby raccoon could, seeing her mother chased into a metal cage with two police dogs nipping at her heels. Her mother turned and looked at Rochelle. "It will be all right, Honey. Don't be afraid. Everything will be all right, Rochelle," her mother called out to her. The cage was placed between the dogs in the back of the truck, and away it sped into the night. Racing after the truck, Rochelle's short legs finally gave way and there she fell to the ground, sobbing. "What have I done? What has happened?" she repeated between the sobs that echoed through a still, dark forest. "Where are you, Mama?"

She hid her eyes with small tear-soaked paws, her little body trembling in exhausted anguish, as a distant noise was lost in her sobs.

The sound of flapping wings grew louder and louder. Jerking her head up and rubbing her eyes, Rochelle trembled as a large winged creature came swooping down, grabbing her fur with its claws and scooping her tiny body up into the night air. All Rochelle could do was scream, as a car sped over the place where she had just been laying. The silhouette of the flapping wings was all she could see against the bright moon. "I'm going to die," she wailed. "No, Child, you are going to live and everything will work out, you'll see," whispered a gentle voice just above her head. A moment of calm swept over Rochelle, who was only to be jarred into fear again, as she soared beneath the flapping wings right into a huge, hollow redwood tree.

"Going down!" hooted her rescuer and the small raccoon found herself flying inside a redwood tree. Rochelle closed her eyes as she was swept through the burned-out tree, into a crevice between massive boulders supporting the tree, and she found herself in a huge cavern. Looking up, she realized that the claws holding fast to her fur belonged to a very large owl. Screaming and fighting, "I want my Mama! Please, it's my fault! I was hungry. Please!" Rochelle found herself being gently placed on a soft twig nest, which reminded her of home. Looking up into the eyes of her rescuer she wondered who was this owl perched before her? To Rochelle, the owl's eyes seemed kind and sincere, not scary and mean. Could this owl be trusted, the little raccoon wondered?

I should act like a big raccoon, thought Rochelle, and she gave it her best. "I don't think I can cry anymore," Rochelle announced, but her loneliness was too great for her to be a big raccoon. She screamed out for her mother. "I miss my mama. Where is she? Please!" Rochelle keenly observed the wise old owl, which gave a slight smile and spoke quietly. "Sweetie, my name is Olivia, and I know you miss your mama. I am here to help you until you are able to be with your mama again." Rochelle's eyes grew large and teary, watching Olivia pull out some fish from between two large stones. Olivia hooted on, "Now, I imagine you might be a bit hungry. What do you think?" "I think I miss my mama, and I want to go home!" Rochelle yelled with such firmness, the owl went silent and placed a small piece of fish near the little raccoon, and slowly Rochelle reached over to pick it up. The little raccoon darted glances around the cavern and at Olivia. "I think your name is Rochelle. Am I right about that?" Nodding yes, Rochelle took a bite of fish.

Rochelle began answering questions. Question after question was asked of the little raccoon-questions about her mother and the way Rochelle was treated. Apparently Olivia was pleased with Rochelle's responses and the physical well-being of her charge, for the small raccoon was met with the caress of a wing, which gave her courage to ask, "What is this place, Olivia?"

Olivia wiped away a tear still clinging to Rochelle's fur. "This, child, is the Haven Lake Crisis Center; a very special place that helps all the forest animals who are in need." "Like me?" Rochelle asked as another thought of her mama being placed in a cage brought fresh tears to be swept away. "Yes, Sweetie, like you, and you need to know that I am going to keep you safe while your mama is away, okay?" Olivia said with a gentle look. "Okay, but where is my mama and why did they take her away?" Rochelle watched Olivia gaze down. "Your mother brought you too close to the humans, and she took food from their containers." "We're so sorry. Please, I want my Mama." Rochelle said. Suddenly very tired, Rochelle looked deep into the eyes of the owl, circled around the nest, nestled into a curled position and closed her eyes. Something in the tone of Olivia's voice was reassuring Rochelle that things could wait until morning. Rochelle peeked up at the old owl moving towards her stone perch to work on Rochelle's paperwork; which in the forest is called barkwork, "Olivia," murmured the little raccoon. "Yes, child?" Olivia whispered. "Thank you," said the tiny animal and with that, Rochelle drifted off to sleep.

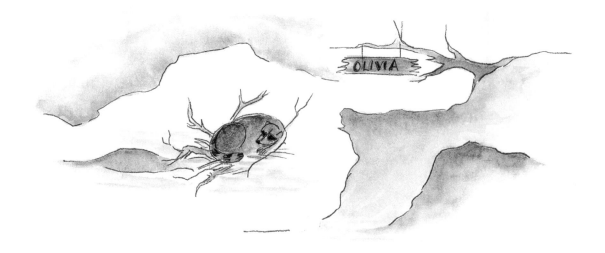

CHAPTER II

The cavern came alive as the day shift came to work, and Rochelle awakened with a start. The sunrays filtered in, filling the cavern with light. Above her head, to her startled amazement, were rows and rows of bats hanging upside down. They were sleeping after a hard night shift at the crisis center. She noticed one bat smiling at her as it dangled from the ceiling, "Don't be afraid, Child." it said. She forgot her fear for a brief moment, smiling at the bats above her, only to have her fears and loneliness flood her with fresh anguish. There were doves on another ledge, speaking to a group of pigeons about the homeless situation on the paths in the forest.

Moving closer to the ledge outside Olivia's office, Rochelle looked below and saw a pack of dogs. Why, they were just like the dogs that had taken her mother away. "You mean dogs! You vicious, awful creatures!" She growled so loud that the entire pack looked up in her direction. Two of the dogs raced, making their way up towards the ledge. Rochelle shook in fear and backed into Olivia's office as the dogs approached her. "Child, what is wrong?" barked the first dog. "Are you okay, little one?" asked the other. They moved closer to see if she was hurt. "Don't touch me!" Rochelle screamed as she reached out to scratch the dog's nose. The big hairy dog lowered itself to the ground to help calm the little raccoon, as the other dog sat down. Both looked at each other and then at Rochelle. "You don't have to be afraid of us, Rochelle, we're police dogs."

Just then Olivia flew into the office. "What is this commotion? Rochelle, these are your friends. They are here to protect you." "These kind took my mother away!" Rochelle snarled. "Who is her mother, Olivia?" asked Officer Scout, the big hairy dog. "She is the raccoon that was caught taking food from the garbage cans." Olivia said, while putting her wing around Rochelle. "Oh, I heard about that one last night. Good rescue, Oli." Olivia smiled, and Rochelle glared as the two dogs left the office, saying goodbye to Rochelle. "Not everyone is unkind, Rochelle. All of these animals are here to help you, your mama, and all of the forest animals." Rochelle was not so sure about the police dogs, but they seemed nice. Rochelle was given a stuffed toy human to play with while Olivia explained to her what had happened to her mother. She discovered that her mama was being held at the Animal Detention Center on the outskirts of the forest. It was a place where animals were jailed, others were hospitalized, and others were there for rehabilitation. Rochelle's only focus was her mama and when she would be with her again.

The Haven Lake Crisis Center was a hopping place. Rochelle saw rabbits being counseled in the parenthood wing of the cavern. The intern owls that were fluttering around Olivia trying to have questions answered regarding their individual cases intrigued the little raccoon. Rochelle giggled with surprise, as she observed the owls being able to watch their young clients and discuss cases at the same time because their heads could spin around. Several small bear cubs got into a tussle over who could play with a stuffed human doll first. Rochelle put aside her toy and went in search of Olivia. She waddled outside Olivia's office smacking right into a baby cub, who stood up on his back legs, roared a baby bear roar, and lowering himself, took a swipe at her with his paw. Rochelle screamed

at the sight of the bear paw causing a daddy long-legs spider and a huge hairy tarantula that were manning the crisis hotlines, to spill the cups of hot lake water they were drinking.

Suddenly there were long and hairy legs moving swiftly in the direction of Rochelle and motioning the baby bear away from her. The little raccoon became dizzy at the commotion of bears, spiders, tarantulas, owls, dogs, and bats. "Barnett, you know better than to hit a girl!" said the daddy long-leg spider, who attempted to hold the bear back. It was an impossible scene, yet Barnett growled and snarled an apology at Rochelle. "Son, you get too angry, and it's going to get you into trouble." she heard the tarantula say as the bear cub waddled away from Rochelle, who stood trembling from such a fierce encounter. "Don't mind that Barnett, Little One. He wouldn't hurt you."

Rochelle's saucer-sized eyes grew even larger as she listened to the smiling tarantula. She had only heard of tarantulas but had never seen one. She watched as he returned to his phones, "Yes, sir, we will send a rescue team right away. Stay on the line and I'll get the directions. You say there is a swarm of bees chasing you, and you have a beehive stuck on your head? We will get on it right away, Mr. Bear." Rochelle was amazed at all the animals that were being helped. She overheard him talking about a lost squirrel being found, an elderly pigeon that had forgotten how to get home, and one of the owls took him home. It was at this time that a squirrel came and took Rochelle to the medical ward of the clinic. Rochelle received a physical examination and Doctor Mole reported she was in great health. The raccoon loved Doctor Mole's glasses and very long nose. She watched as birds of all shapes and sizes checked the enormous Haven Lake Forest map on the stone wall, and then flew away to deliver messages from all over the forest, especially near Haven Lake. Rochelle listened as Olivia explained how many of the forest children were placed with foster families around Haven Lake, and this was where Olivia decided to place Rochelle.

Sitting Rochelle down, Olivia explained how every forest child needed a safe place to stay until they could be reunited with their parent. Insisting that she would be just fine staying at the crisis center, Rochelle began to cry, not knowing where she would now be sent. "Please Olivia, let me stay with you." Rochelle whimpered. "Sweetie, staying with me is not the best for you. I will be your caseworker. Remember, I told you I would make sure you were safe until you are with your mama again, and I will."

Rochelle did remember, and with the flapping of wings, she was speeding through the crevice, the hollow limb, and up the redwood tree. Soaring across the trees, the majestic blue Haven Lake was in plain view. They headed south over the tall redwoods and crystal water towards the south end of the lake. A large branch and twig-filled dam blocked the run off of the lake. They had arrived at her new foster home. Rochelle looked around at the sawed-off tree stumps. "What is this place?" Rochelle asked as she scurried along the ground until Olivia released her claws.

A strong chippy voice rang out, "This is timber country, Little Lady." She turned to face a huge bucktoothed beaver answering her. Startled, she covered her eyes and began to cry. "Now, now, Dear... don't let Mr. Beaver frighten you," said Mrs. Beaver. Rochelle moved her paws away just enough to see a sweet-faced beaver coming towards her and Olivia. The little raccoon had never been face to face with a beaver before, so she backed right against Olivia as she listened to Mrs. Beaver. "I am Mrs. Beaver, and I am so happy you are going to spend time with us, Dear. Why, Olivia told us all about you, Sweetie, and I think you will like staying with us, won't she, Dear?" said Mrs. Beaver, smiling while turning in the direction of her husband. Rochelle jumped at the sound of Mr. Beaver's loud voice. "Yes indeed, Dear. Now I have some wood to chuck, and we should introduce Rochelle to the other children." Mr. Beaver began to thump his huge flat tail on the ground, and Rochelle stood feeling the ground move with every thump, waiting for the others to greet her.

The smell of fresh wood filled the air, and the sound of the water caressing the lake's shore reminded Rochelle of all the lake walks she took with her mother. Her mother! It was all her fault that she had been caught for stealing. Rochelle had made all the noise. She missed her mama, and without warning, Rochelle began to sob. The loneliness and longing were almost unbearable. If only she hadn't been so noisy. If only she hadn't been hungry and begging her mother for something to eat, rather than waiting until they were down by the lake. If only she hadn't whined. The thoughts thundered through Rochelle's mind, and the sobbing grew louder. Not even Olivia could sooth the torment that raged within. The guilt and longing were too great to be comforted.

"Stop crying! Stop!" Rochelle looked through her tears to see a tiny gray rat with a long, slender tail, yelling and racing toward her as fast as possible. "The more upset you get the worse it will be for all of us." Suddenly, a little black and white animal came out from behind a stump. "Why is she crying, Alto?" said the nervous creature. Rochelle looked at the rat, then at the other creature and she burst into a new set of sobs. Rochelle felt the rat's paw in hers, as he shook it fast. "My name is Alto, and Odiferus gets upset when anyone else is upset. Please, I'm begging you to stop crying!"

Rochelle watched as Odiferus began to tear up. Soon he was crying too, and Alto was yelling for everyone to run for cover. The little raccoon hid under Olivia's wing, but as she inhaled for another set of strong sobs, Rochelle gagged. What was that awful smell? Ugh! It was terrible, and she looked over at Odiferus, who was sobbing as loud as she had been, but his tail stood straight up. She covered her nose with her paws, "What is that smell?" She asked Alto. As all of them watched Odiferus from a distance, Alto explained, "Odiferus is a skunk, Rochelle, and every time someone else is upset, well, he gets upset too. The rest is nose history." "Oh my, I am sorry, Odiferus," said Rochelle, and she watched as the skunk went back to the stump he had been hiding behind.

Rochelle stopped crying, and Mr. Beaver thumped again, calling Odiferus and the others to return to meet the little raccoon. A little bear cub came lumbering towards Rochelle, "Hi, I'm Barnett," he said and then they recognized one another, "Hey, I remember you from the crisis center," said the bear. Rochelle cautiously nodded her acknowledgement. Alto began to introduce the others to Rochelle as she watched the final foster child totter over near Rochelle. "And this is Quilla, said Alto, she is a porcupine and very shy." Rochelle watched as Quilla stood between Mr. and Mrs. Beaver. Her quills stood straight up all over her body. "Hello" said Rochelle, but Quilla only nodded. Barnett moved closer. "Never give her a hug. I gave her a bear hug once and it took us days to remove the quills!" Rochelle looked back and forth between Barnett and Quilla, shuddering at the painful thought of having a quill in her paw or fur. She looked at her surroundings and looked up at Olivia, "I am ready to return to the crisis center, Olivia," Rochelle stated. Olivia told her she would be fine, and she would see her in two days, and with a final farewell to all, Olivia flew northwest over Haven Lake, leaving Rochelle gazing out over the water as Olivia became only a speck and then was gone.

CHAPTER III

Rochelle had little time for tears because between Mrs. Beaver and Alto talking to her, she could only concentrate on what they were saying. She would be hollow-mates with Quilla in the upstairs portion of the dam. It was a lovely branch room with a bunk bed of bark and twigs. Quilla would sleep on the top bunk because of her quills. Rochelle was fine with that. There was a small window in the ceiling and one facing the lake. It had just enough room for them to move around without someone getting pricked.

Rochelle looked out the window and saw a huge redwood tree near the dam and water's edge. As she stepped out to approach the tree, a pinecone hit her on the head. "Hey, ouch, that hurt!" she yelled. "This is the guys' hollow. Stay out!" yelled Barnett with a roar. "Well, fine!" Rochelle yelled back, and began moving away, until she heard Alto giggling. She looked into the hollow just in time to see Alto slide down Barnett's side, landing with a small thud on the ground. Alto giggled again. "What is that all around your mouth?" Rochelle asked.

Alto laughed and swayed a bit. "Nothing but berry juice, fly?" The raccoon looked at him funny. "What do you mean, fly?" Barnett pushed Alto aside with one swift smack of his paw, "He meant, why!" "What's wrong with him?" Rochelle questioned as she watched Alto wrap himself up in his tail and then fall over when he tried to walk. "He likes to eat too many red berries," Barnett said with a sigh.

"I see," Rochelle whispered back. Soon Alto was sound asleep still wrapped up in his tail. Rochelle watched as Barnett gently scooped Alto up into his paw and placed Alto on his small bed hollowed out within the tree trunk. She knew they were friends. "Would you like to take a walk?" Rochelle asked Barnett and he growled "yes."

Along the stream they strolled, and Rochelle realized that she was small enough to walk right under Barnett's belly. The thought made her smile. One time she was small enough to walk under her mama's belly. A lump grew in her throat and she began to cry. Barnett turned and Rochelle looked up at him with big tears in her eyes. Rochelle leaped out of the way as Barnett went into a screaming rage.

He smashed at the branches. He thrashed at the tree trunks with his sharp claws, and he smacked the water, slipping on a mossy stone and flying headlong into the lake. She watched in amazement as he slipped beneath the water, and then came flying up roaring so loud that the birds flew from the trees. Rochelle had stopped crying simply due to being so startled. Barnett's wet matted fur dripped with water and mud. His eyes were squinted with rage, and he sat in the water sobbing. "I'm sorry your mother isn't with you, Rochelle." He moved towards the shore, only to slip again and land back under the water, smashing and thrashing in rage.

Finally, Rochelle moved to the edge of the water. "Barnett, please calm down and come to shore. We can talk about this. Okay?" Rochelle said as she peered over a rock she was hidden behind. Barnett came ashore, shaking off the water and mud. He sniffed back tears and sat down near Rochelle's rock. "I'm okay now." He said. "I just get so angry when someone hurts." Rochelle moved closer to him. "To be so angry, you must hurt too," she said. Rochelle was about to learn just how hurt Barnett was as he began his story.

"They killed my dad!" he sobbed. "Who killed your dad?" Rochelle asked in horror. "Humans and police dogs! I was there and saw the whole thing!" He cried as he pounded the ground. Rochelle put her small paw on his large paw. "I'm so sorry. What happened?" she asked, placing her paw on his arm. "My dad and I were walking through the forest picnic area for humans. Dad saw a car with food inside. He tried to get in and got very angry. Dad pounded on a window and broke it, then roared when humans came near. He climbed into the car window and got stuck, roaring even louder because he was so angry. I roared too, to keep the humans back. I saw them coming with guns! The humans saw that my dad was stuck, so they shot him. He went limp in the car and they dragged him out, throwing him into the back of a truck. Big dogs started chasing me, and I ran and ran. The dogs were called back, but I kept running. I ran all night. Rochelle, they killed my dad!" He shook his head, and tears ran down his furry cheeks.

"As the sun came up, I came upon a beehive in an old log hanging over the water at Willow Springs. Several bees saw me coming and came after me! I became so enraged at their constant buzzing that I charged for the log, slipped and flew right into the spring water. I came up slapping the water, bees, and air, crying and roaring! Then I heard a strong voice above me say, 'That is quite enough!' and that is when I met...". Rochelle said her name at the same time Barnett finished his sentence, "Olivia." Rochelle watched, as she gave a faint giggle, Barnett sort of smiled and then turned angry once again. "Olivia took me to the beehive and gave me honey. The bees were quite nice to her and me. She took me to the Haven Lake Crisis Center. Wow! What a place that is! Anyway, she found out from the police dogs that my father was alive, but I don't believe her. I don't believe anybody!" he roared. Rochelle backed away a bit. "My father is dead and now I live with beavers!" He stood on his hind legs and roared to the sky. His pain was so great, and Rochelle could do nothing.

All of a sudden she heard flapping of wings, and there she was, Olivia! The owl swooped onto a perch just above their heads. "I said I would be back in two days, and here it has only been two hours and I get a call! Barnett, I have been looking for you." Rochelle hid behind Barnett thinking that Olivia was only looking for him. "Rochelle." The little raccoon moved so she could see the owl, while still hiding. "You must never leave your foster home without telling Mr. or Mrs. Beaver where you are going. Barnett, you know better. You must be careful because of the wolves!"

Rochelle remembered her mama telling her about the wolves. They run in packs and are very vicious, always looking for trouble. "We're sorry, Olivia." Rochelle stated, but Barnett only growled. "Oh, and Barnett, I spoke with your father this afternoon. He is in anger management classes now," Olivia shared. Barnett looked up at her. "He is dead!" he roared. Olivia just shook her head, telling them both to return to the dam, and she followed them back, Rochelle following close behind Barnett. Rochelle missed the protection of her mother. She grew very silent as the loneliness swept in like the darkness. It was getting dark and the howling of wolves could be heard in the distance.

CHAPTER IV

Fireflies brightened the small hollows of the dam. The sounds of the night were in fine chorus, and there stood the beavers. Mr. Beaver's tail was thumping nervously and Rochelle saw Mrs. Beaver putting her paws up to her head. "Children, children, you must tell us where you are going. We worry so much when you wander away." said Mrs. Beaver. Rochelle quietly said, "I'm sorry. I didn't realize how far we had walked or how late it was getting." The little raccoon watched as Olivia cleared her throat loud enough, and nudged Barnett hard enough for him to growl an apology too. Rochelle smirked under her breath at the sight, and after saying goodnight to everyone she headed for her hollow. As she climbed the branches of the dam, Rochelle looked up at the bright moon, which cast a glistening light on Haven Lake. Could her mama see the moon, she wondered? The tears that were always so close to the surface bubbled to the top and ran down her cheeks. "I miss you and love you, Mama! Goodnight!" she shouted to the sky, and then moved over the sturdy branches to the hole, which led to her hollow.

Rochelle heard soft sobbing coming from the top bunk. "Quilla, are you all right?" she whispered. The quills stood straight up on Quilla's back. "Leave me alone!" Quilla snarled. "You seem very sad." Rochelle responded. Quilla turned her head to face Rochelle, and by the light of the fireflies Rochelle saw the anger and sadness in the porcupine's eyes. "I have a counselor to help me, and I have Mr. and Mrs. Beaver! Now leave me alone!" Quilla demanded. Rochelle felt lonely all of a sudden and curled up on her bunk nest. "I'm sorry, Quilla." she said, and as the fireflies slowly drifted out of the hollow, Rochelle fell into a restless sleep, dreaming of her mother.

"Ouch!" yelled Rochelle waking with a start. She rubbed her backside and realized that Quilla had accidentally backed into her as she got off her bunk. "Oh, I'm sorry," stated Quilla, "I'm late for my counseling session at the crisis center." She toddled out of the hollow as fast as her little legs could carry her. "You must always be on time for session!" she yelled as she disappeared over the branches. Rochelle growled a bit as she continued to rub her backside. It was her first full day at Crystal Cove, home of the beavers' dam, and a place she hoped her mama would be able to find one day.

Mr. Beaver was chucking wood and having Alto and Barnett assist him with chores. Mrs. Beaver was in the water rearranging branches. Rochelle watched Alto move towards her as she waddled down to the water to wash her face. She was hungry.

"Good morning!" Alto yelled as he raced up to her. "I'll bet you're hungry. Hey, I know where you can get some awesome berries." Alto jumped and pointed in the direction heading north around the cove. Rochelle giggled at the sight of a jumping rat. "No thank you. I saw what those berries do for you," she said smiling. Alto gave a sheepish grin, "I like my berries...just like my old man!" "Who is that?" Rochelle questioned. "Oh, I mean my father. Yeah, he is the father of all fathers...that's my old man. I wanna be just like him!" yelled Alto in a deep phony voice. "Come with me," Alto said as he yelled over to Mr. Beaver. "Hey, Mr. Beaver, can I take Rochelle along the cove for breakfast?" Two solid thumps on the ground could be heard, which confused Rochelle until Alto explained that when Mr. Beaver was chucking wood, he would only answer in thumps. One thump meant no, and two thumps meant yes.

So, off they headed along the waterfront, Rochelle watched for small minnows so she could snatch them up for breakfast. Alto talked a mile a minute as he raced back and forth across the trail. Finally Rochelle placed her paw on his tail. Needless to say, his legs kept running until he realized he was going nowhere. "Hey! What are you doing?" he squealed. She gave a little laugh and said, "Alto, you must slow down so I can understand everything you are saying. Have you had any berries this morning?" Rochelle wondered why he was so excited. "No berries yet!"

said Alto with a grin. "How did you end up here with the beavers, Alto?" Rochelle asked as she snatched another small fish from the water. "Oh, that's a long story. You see I have been in a lot of foster homes." Alto said as he swung from a branch with his tail. "My dad is in rehab at the detention center because he gets drunk on berries." Rochelle looked at him hanging upside down. "You mean the berries you eat are what put your father in the detention center?" The little raccoon was quite taken aback. "Yeah," said Alto "My old man couldn't handle eating the berries, so they tossed him in the center to get better. They call getting better, rehabilitation, which is too long of a word for me! He giggled. Anyway, I love my berries and I can handle it!" Rochelle shook her head in amazement, knowing better. "How many foster homes have you been in?" She asked, and so began the long tale of Alto's foster homes.

"Well," he began, "First Olivia put me with the Buzzard family. They were very nice folks, but they couldn't cook, so we ate out a lot, mostly at roadside stops. It was gross! That was when Olivia had just become a crisis worker and my old man was sent to rehab." "Were you scared?" asked Rochelle. "Nope, I just missed my dad a lot. That is when I started eating berries." Alto said in a serious voice, then he got silly. "The next family was way cool."

"The squirrel family had a great home, and I was kept busy doing chores for them. In fact, it was wild. Those folks just work, work, and work. They are always storing nuts for the winter. I carried nuts all day and filled all sorts of places with nuts. Fact is, it drove me nuts! Olivia then took me to live with the dove family, but they were so lovey-dovey with each other, they forgot I was around, and I got into the berries for good. Now I'm here with the Beavers, and they're the best foster folks I've ever had, but I' m still doing the berries. I just love them." Alto shouted at the top of his lungs and twirled around on his tail. Rochelle laughed at such a sight, but felt sorry for Alto and she looked sad. "Hey, don't feel sad for me," Alto smiled, "all of the foster parents have been cool. My dad is coming back for me as soon as he gets out of the rehab center, and Olivia assigned a really cool rat named Rudy, who is helping me kick my habit. Soon the berries will be history, Rudy says, and I will be able to be happy without them! Ha, I wanna be just like my old man!" thundered the little gray rat, as Rochelle watched him run up the side of a boulder and do a flip on to the ground. Rochelle laughed and clapped her paws together to applaud Alto's feat. She knew they would be good friends and knew the berries would have to go. Alto knew this too, but right now he twirled around his new friend.

CHAPTER V

Rochelle forced herself to keep busy as the days passed, and still her mother did not come to find her. She enjoyed her new friends, although it was hard to befriend Quilla. Rochelle would watch as Quilla followed the beavers everywhere they went. Quilla would rarely speak, and trusted no one, even when Rochelle was being nice to her.

And then there was Odiferus, who was so very nervous and shy. Rochelle liked his little smile, but she had to be very careful not to upset him. Odiferus was always getting upset, crying, and, well, smelling, Rochelle thought to herself. It would be hours before the smell would lessen and she could talk with him again.

One evening, Rochelle filled with anger when Quilla said something mean about Rochelle never being able to see her mother again. Rochelle raced out of their hollow and tripped on a root. She found herself tumbling down the side of the dam and right into Odiferus' hollow in the rocks.

"Oh my," said Odiferus, "you have come to visit me!" Rochelle looked up at his little smiling face, hoping that he wasn't too startled. The air remained fresh and the fireflies lit up the cozy little rock hollow. It was a perfect place for Odiferus, Rochelle thought. Rochelle said with a smile, "Here I am."

Odiferus was pleased to have her company. Rochelle wondered where his mother could be all this time, so she asked. Odiferus blew a firefly from off his nose and spoke in a very soft whisper. Rochelle had to lean closer to hear him speak. "My mother was hit by a car." "What!" Rochelle stated louder than she expected. Fireflies scattered and Odiferus' tail began to stretch out. "No, no, it's okay!" Rochelle said in a calming voice, and that did the trick, for Odiferus calmed down. "Please

16

tell me what happened," she asked as she curled up near the hollow entranceway, mainly for the fresh air coming off the lake.

Odiferus began to talk of his mother, telling Rochelle funny stories of growing up with her. He loved the scent of his mom, and became dreamy as he recalled the songs she sang to him in the evening. Rochelle laughed and enjoyed hearing him sing a song his mom would make up. "My sweet little Odiferus, a bundle of love...you are my little angel scent from above." A tear fell from his eye as he looked out at the lake beyond Rochelle. Rochelle looked into his eyes and he blushed while wiping the tears with his paws. "Boy skunks don't cry," he said, blowing several fire-flies away so he could hide in the dark. "Everyone cries," Rochelle gently said. "Olivia says it's okay to cry because we miss our parents and are scared. "Tell me what happened to your mom," she asked and Odiferus began to talk.

"I hate the big road with the line down the center." He said. "My mom always said not to walk on roads unless it is necessary. Well, one night it was very necessary." Rochelle watched, as his eyes grew big. "The wolves were after us." He whispered. "We could hear them running just above, on Howling Ridge. Mom had told me to run, but I wanted to spray them blind. I would protect my mother." He said as he sat up proudly, only to sink into a slump. "The wolves grew closer and the time I wasted," he began to cry, "caused my mom to make a serious decision." Rochelle tried to comfort him, but it was useless. He swallowed hard and continued, "She pushed me in front of her and yelled for me to run straight across the road. Just as the wolves reached the road, bright lights came zooming by, and then there were many bright lights. I turned and the wolves were gone, the bright lights were gone, and in the moonlight..." Odiferus stopped speaking, and then whispered, "There was my mom lying on the road. She was very still."

Rochelle could not speak. She felt the familiar ache in her heart, a pain that even Olivia could not soothe. She knew he felt it too. She held back her sobs but the tears streamed down her fur as Odiferus continued his story. "I slowly moved back towards my Mom, calling her name, and finally that scent, that wonderful scent filled the air. She moved her head towards me and said she was hurt very bad.

My mom told me to go get help, so I headed in the direction of the bright lights and came to a yard where there were some dogs." Rochelle trembled at the thought of dogs, any dogs. Odiferus looked at her and began to tremble too. "No," Rochelle whispered, "I'm all right. What did you do?" Odiferus explained how the dogs were really gruff at first, until his tail went up and then they barked for one of the neighborhood police dogs. "His name was Officer Scout," he firmly said in an admiring way. "Officer Scout told me that he would find my mom and get her help. That was the last time I saw my mother." Odiferus said, looking down at his paws. "I was told to stay where I was with two other police dogs until Olivia arrived. They were very nice to me, but weren't too keen about standing close to me. I miss being hugged by my mom." He sobbed out the words and a scent filled the room that caused the fireflies to exit, but Rochelle took a deep breath of fresh lake air and stayed with him until he fell asleep in his tears. Rochelle missed her mama so badly she decided it was time to find her. She had to think of a plan. So as she held the smelly little skunk in her arms the plan began to take form. Rochelle would not cry another tear, she determined. She had a plan!

CHAPTER VI

"Good morning, Mrs. Beaver," spoke Rochelle. She kept her eyes on Mrs. Beaver, as Rochelle washed her face down by the water's edge. Waddling over to help Mrs. Beaver with some branches she was adding to the dam, the little raccoon decided to ask her a question. "Mrs. Beaver, where is the Animal Detention Center?" she asked in a matter-of-fact sort of way. "Oh dear, Rochelle, you don't want to go there, Sweetie. It is below Howling Ridge and across the road. If you want to visit your mother, you need to talk with Olivia, Dear." "Sure." Rochelle murmured in a soft, long sigh. Olivia had promised she could see her mother soon, but she wanted to see her now! How she longed to see her mother's smile and the twinkling of her eyes, as she would stroke Rochelle's fur!

Rochelle enjoyed seeing Olivia at her counseling sessions with the wise old owl, but missing her mother was just becoming too hard. She had to act on her plan before Mrs. Beaver could talk to Olivia, Rochelle thought. She would get Alto, Barnett, and Odiferous to help her. In fact, she might even persuade Quilla to join her too. Rochelle's mind raced as she waddled away from Mrs. Beaver, in search of Alto, Barnett, Odiferus, and Quilla. She spotted the group down by the cove and ran in their direction. The plan would work for all five of us, she reasoned in her mind, and they could do it tonight.

"Are you out of your mind!" Barnett roared, scaring a group of butterflies as he smashed his way through the high grass along the cove. He continued to slap the grass and fling clumps of dirt into the calm water's edge.

"Honestly, Barnett, you have got to chill out," Alto voiced as he peeled back a piece of berry skin, popping the berry in his mouth and smacking his lips. Rochelle just rolled her eyes, as Odiferus was testing his fear barometer of a tail regarding this adventure. "I am afraid of the dark!" He exclaimed with saucer eyes staring at Rochelle. "How can you be afraid of the dark, when you are nocturnal?" asked the disgusted raccoon. "I am not nocturnal, I am skunkturnal!" He stated with great pride. "You don't even know what nocturnal means!" yelled Rochelle, getting up to leave. "I do so!" he quivered. "Oh really" she said as she turned to waddle away, "then you would know that you aren't supposed to be afraid of the dark, but can move around at night if you want!" Rochelle snarled, starting off into the high grass to find something to eat. "Hey, don't go! You have a great plan!" Odiferus yelled after her, and the others joined in agreement, causing her to turn around. "None of you know what the plan is," she said lowering her eyebrows as only a raccoon can do. "True" said Quilla, "but anyone who knows the meaning of nocturnal must have a great plan!" The rest nodded in agreement, as Barnett came to sit next to Alto and accidentally stepped on his long tail. "Yeeooooooowwwwwwww," Alto wailed as Barnett jumped back, and the rat instantly had his tail tip in his mouth. "Now that is just wrong! WRONG, I say!" yelled Alto as he rocked himself against a tree, holding his tail like a baby. "Sorry," quietly said Barnett, and everyone looked at him in astonishment. Rochelle continued to look at Barnett in amazement as she told everyone about her plan.

Speaking in a whisper, no louder than the swaying high grass in the cove, Rochelle began again. "We can leave tonight, just after the fireflies come out. The stars and moon will be bright enough, and we can leave for the Animal Detention Center. Once we are there, we can rescue our parents, set them free, run into the forest and live happily ever after." She gazed off in a dreamy state, until Alto brought her back to reality. "Hey, dreamer, are you forgetting the distance to the detention center, the road crossing near the detention center, breaking into the detention center, the police dogs at the detention center, and..?!" Odiferus loudly interrupted with two words that made each of them shudder, "the wolves!" In that moment, without even thinking about it, everyone got up and moved upwind from Odiferus.

"Will you come with me tonight just after the fireflies come out?" Rochelle asked while searching their eyes for an answer. "I want to be with my mama." She trembled, determined to hold back the tears. Everyone nodded as Rochelle put out her little paw, only to have a smaller skunk paw, then a rat paw, and finally a huge bear cub paw wrap itself around the others. Quilla stood off a bit. "I don't think I can do this. There is no one at the Animal Detention Center that I want to see." Rochelle turned in her direction. "No one," she questioned? "No one. I have no parents." Quilla said, as she looked at the ground. Each looked at the other.

"Then come with us, anyway. We are family now, and your quills could help keep us safe." Said Alto, as he was still rubbing his tail. "I'm not your family. Why should I care if you are safe or not?" growled Quilla as her quills began to straighten up. "I'm staying with Mr. and Mrs. Beaver. In fact, I'm going to tell on all of you. You know you are not to leave the foster home."

Quilla began to move towards the dam, and in two strides Barnett was blocking her path. "Get out of my way, Barnett! You've already had a nose full of my quills before!" "Yes" said Barnett," but this time I don't care! We've all been nice to you, and you're always so mean. We have tried to be a friend to you, and you are always rude and angry. We need your help, and you don't even care! I don't care what has made you like this, but right now we are the only family you have who cares about you, and we need your help! So, so shame on you!" Barnett's voice went soft on the last statement, and he sighed. Again, everyone looked at Barnett in astonishment, including Quilla. He shrugged his black shoulders and snarled, "I guess counseling is working."

All of a sudden Quilla began to giggle, and then laughed. Barnett started to chuckle and pretty soon the forest rang out with the laughter of a strong band of new friends ready to begin their adventure, even though Quilla continued to keep a safe distance from the others. The plan was set as they moved through the high grasses towards the dam they called home. They would wait for the fireflies.

CHAPTER VII

"The fireflies...would they ever come?" Rochelle thought as she watched the sun slowly fall into Haven Lake's shimmering waves. She could still hear Mr. Beaver felling the smaller bushy trees near the huge dam. The sounds of dragging tree branches would only be interrupted with an occasional rant from Barnett or a loud thumping of Mr. Beaver's wide flat tail.

Rochelle gazed back at the dam from the small bluff where she sat grooming herself, after eating several small minnows. She watched as Quilla followed Mrs. Beaver around like a shadow. Only when Mrs. Beaver slipped into the water of Crystal Cove, to place branches on the dam, did Quilla sit on the water's edge. She would approach the water as if she was a beaver, until her paws got wet, and then Quilla would once again be a porcupine, with her quills standing straight up in disgust.

Alto's yells caught Rochelle's attention, as she shockingly saw him flying through the air, and then landing with a splash in the cove. Swimming to shore, he was muttering to himself. Apparently he had found a nice place to snooze on a fallen branch, only to be hurled into the water as Barnett lifted the branch for Mr. Beaver. Barnett chuckled, but Odiferus was rolling with laughter. It was the first time Rochelle ever saw a skunk rolling, but then it was the first time she ever saw a flying rat. The little raccoon tried to look very serious as Alto passed by her, shaking off the water that matted his gray fur. She let a tiny squeak of a giggle slip through her lips, and Alto shot her the meanest look he could make dripping wet. She returned to looking out over the bluff. Out there was her mother, and tonight she was going to find her, no matter what! She closed her eyes for a moment, and then she saw it.

One flicker of light was shining bright in the high grass. The first firefly joined the evening light. "Hello, my friend." Rochelle sighed. Night was almost upon them, and all in the forest stopped their work and play. The small raccoon peered out over the bluff to watch as birds began to settle in their trees and bushes. The deer wandered down to the water's edge for water and greens. It was suppertime at Haven Lake, and the cove was cast in the evening sky's dark blues and crimson colors, becoming darker as the sun disappeared into the lake.

Rochelle listened to the choir of frogs and crickets singing their favorite forest tunes. Soon the fireflies began to dance as the unique croaking of those who sang best echoed over the smooth glassy lake. Off the raccoon waddled to gather her fellow conspirators. Mr. and Mrs. Beaver would soon be heading for their nest after making sure each of their foster forest children were tucked into their nests and nooks. Rochelle watched with Quilla, as the beavers slipped into the water, entering their home, which was above the water's edge within the dam. Their five forest children waited until the sky filled with stars and fireflies. Only then were the sweet snores of Mr. and Mrs. Beaver heard. They were wonderful foster parents, and they trusted Rochelle, Barnett, Alto, Odiferus, and Quilla. And that trust would be sadly broken this very night.

CHAPTER VIII

One by one, each little critter crept from his nest or nook being amazingly quiet for such a noisy bunch. They almost stepped in pace with each snore that came from within the dam. The odd little group of forest children moved carefully towards the small path that would lead them to Howling Ridge. Only nocturnal creatures could maneuver the branches and roots that crossed the winding path. Up and up they moved, on the twisting and turning path, as they slowly made their way to the ridge.

Off in the distance a terrible sound could be heard, which caused Barnett to stop in his tracks. Rochelle, Alto, and Odiferus backed up against Barnett. "Hey, you guys," he growled, "stop it!" Everyone, in unison, with the exception of Barnett, breathed the same whisper of a word, "wolves". "I'm sure they are a long way off, chasing down their supper right now, so let's get going and all of you get off of me!" he snarled, trying hard to remain calm. Quilla waited as the others moved away from Barnett with one apology after another, especially Odiferus. On, the small band of animals moved. Quickly moving to Howling Ridge, Alto began to complain about the distance, because his little legs were beginning to throb in pain. "I hate to be a complainer," he said, interrupted by Quilla's sassy comment regarding how he always complains, which was quite untrue. Rochelle shot Quilla a disgusted look, and up went the quills. Rochelle turned to Alto, "Tell me what is wrong, my friend!" Alto smiled at her, and then gave an even broader grin to Quilla, who continued to walk on. "Rochelle, all of you have bigger paws than I do, so I'm taking many more steps than all of you." he said, "Truth is, my legs hurt." For the first time, Rochelle looked down at her small friend and realized how tiny he was. She smiled, and probably for the first time since creation a rat was riding on the back of a raccoon near Howling Ridge by Haven Lake. Of course, that is what friends are for, and hopefully Quilla would realize this fact one day, Rochelle thought, as she continued her efforts to be with her mother.

They were at the edge of Firefly Meadow when out jumped a deer with great antlers, sending the crew scattering in all directions screaming "wolf". "See here, children!" billowed a mighty deer, "I am certainly no wolf! What are you doing in the forest alone?" Behind him came a gentle moving deer with a small fawn behind her. "Now, Buck, don't frighten the children." She sweetly spoke, as she eyed each one. "Children, why are you out so late?" In one breath, each was speaking at the same time, telling the tale of what, where, and why. She listened with great patience until all had become silent and then she sighed, "Oh my." She nuzzled her fawn, and Rochelle asked, "Should we go back?" knowing in her heart what the answer would be. "It would be most wise for all of you to return to Mr. and Mrs. Beaver's dam. When the beavers awake, they will be so worried and surely all of Haven Lake Crisis Center will be in an uproar. I am sure that your parents are fine. Why, I harmed my leg in a grand leap across the road. The rangers came and wrapped my leg, took me to the Animal Detention Center, and soon I was set free here at Firefly Meadow. What a joy to meet Buck in the meadow." She looked up at her husband, who stood strong and brave next to her newborn fawn. She gave them both a loving look and smile. Rochelle and the others turned in the direction of the dam. Heads were low and they slowly thanked the deer as they moved back the way they came. The deer nodded, wishing the children a safe journey back and slowly moved into the forest bushes.

"We can't stop now!" screamed Rochelle at the top of her lungs! She sat down on a small stump. "I won't go back now!" With that scream, bats flew off branches, screeching from the noise coming from below. The others turned to Rochelle and formed a semi-circle around her. The debate was on. Quilla most definitely wanted to go home and was very vocal about it. She had no reason to go on, for her world was with Mr. and Mrs. Beaver. Alto was ashamed he needed to ride on Rochelle's back, so he too was willing to go back to the dam. Rochelle began to tear up. She would go on alone she announced and began to waddle away in the direction of Howling Ridge. She pushed back the tears. "I said NO TEARS!" she yelled to no one, but four friends heard her. "Okay!" They yelled in unison in her direction and moved as a group toward their friend. She turned to see them in the moonlight, and first came a smile. Soon they were all giggling with excitement as they caught up with Rochelle and their new sense of determination. Mrs. Deer was right, but they had to do what they had to do. Soon they were moving fast with Howling Ridge's edge in sight. The ridge overlooked Blue Belly Swamp, a bit of Falcon Gulch, and the lights of the humans in the far distance.

CHAPTER IX

It would be only a matter of time before they would reach the detention center, and the anticipation was great, moving them forward. Moving them quickly forward, only to be stopped in their tracks, frozen to sounds of ... WOLVES! "Run!" wailed Odiferus, and run they did, or perhaps to be more descriptive, rapidly waddled. Alto was hanging onto the fur of Rochelle, and looking like a kite swaying in high wind. His own tail kept smacking him in the face, which for a rat was just wrong. Barnett bounded past his friends and then stopped, standing on his hind legs and waving his arms. "Stop!" he yelled and everyone slammed on his or her brakes, skidding to the edge of Howling Ridge, everyone except for Alto. He lost his grip and went hurtling into the air. His flight astonished the group, putting Rochelle into shock as she watched Alto disappear over the

ridge. They could hear his scream all the way to the bottom of the ridge, and then silence. They all screamed his name at once and moved as fast as they could down the ridge path. It seemed like hours before they reached the bottom, fearful of what they would find. Tears were flying from everyone's eyes. Rochelle, Odiferus, Barnett, and Quilla yelled his name over and over, searching behind rocks, and weeds. Finally, they came to a big metal box. From the box came a familiar voice. "I'm in heaven! I'm truly in heaven!" said Alto. He had landed in a dumpster filled with garbage.

A small path and ledge hung just above the dumpster, so the others managed to climb up and look inside. There, in the moonlight, sat Alto eating a bite of stale bread, still a bit dazed from his first long-distance, airborne flight. They all shook their heads in amazement. Alto was just fine, and now they had the road to conquer. The forest children were almost to their destination. They rested by the dumpster as Alto tossed each of them some of their favorite snacks: old smelly fish bits, cheese mold, some lunch meat gone slightly green, and the lovely meal gave them strength to go on. Finally a branch was lowered for Alto to climb out of the dumpster, and they were again on their way. This time Alto walked. All seemed content and much braver than before the ridge. Now they walked toward the road with a new sense of courage.

Lights reflected on the road, as fast moving traffic whizzed by the forest children that stood at the edge in the high grass. The little forest creatures' eyes were the size of saucers but no lights came from them. All of a sudden, everyone wanted his or her mother, father, or beavers. Each little animal shivered in fear from the great noises coming from the moving traffic. "How do we ever get across this road?" Barnett asked Rochelle. "There must be a way," she said. "We just run for it!" Said Odiferus, and Alto nodded. Quilla was in shock at the sight and was looking like a pincushion. "Okay," Quilla stated, "I'm scared." They all bobbed their heads up and down in agreement, just staring at the cars, trucks, and road that stood before them.

Suddenly from the forest, beside the dumpster, rustling noise could be heard. All heads turned slowly in the direction of the noise. Hearts started to race, and so did legs, as everyone screamed the word of the night, "WOLVES!" and across the road they flew. Not one animal looked in any direction except straight ahead. Cars beeped their horns, trucks weaved around, and a motorcycle flew into a ditch. The man yelled words not worth repeating, but he and his motorcycle were okay. It looked like all were safe, except for Alto, who was run over several times, only to stand and wave. A tire never hit him, and he was short enough to be safe under the moving traffic. They never noticed him, which, after the fact, caused him to be insulted. As they all huddled together checking to see if everyone had all their toes and tails, they saw sets of eyes moving from the nearby bushes. Everyone thought they were about to die, when from the grasses came Mrs. Opossum with her babies hanging on her sides.

They all squealed hello, and the forest children looked at each other and began rolling in the high grass alongside the road, laughing in amazing relief.

Mrs. Opossum was concerned for the children too, as her own little ones climbed all over the others, with the exception of Quilla and Odiferus, of course. She had not seen the wolves in the area, but traveling without their parents was unsafe, and she shook her head to stress her thoughts to them. Quilla explained what they were doing out so late, and although Mrs. Opossum seemed to understand, she felt it was necessary to report the children to the Haven Lake Crisis Center as soon as she got her children home safely to their hollow. This meant they would have to hurry if they were going to rescue their parents. Hoping that Mrs. Opossum had wandered far from her hollow, they said their goodbyes as she placed her children safely on her sides, and moved away from the direction of the detention center.

Lights glowed from extremely high poles and a very high electric fence surrounded the center. "Oh, dear, how do we get over that fence?" asked Rochelle to anyone listening. They all sat down in the high grass as a single line facing the obstacle. "No problem," said Odiferus approaching the fence, "I can squeeze through.." ZAP! Instantly, they watched in horror as he stiffened and fell backward to the ground. Racing to their friend, he looked up into their eyes and said, "Well that was a shocking experience!" Quilla rolled her eyes and said "Plan B?" Everyone sighed. "My mama is in there." Rochelle whispered in awe. "So is my dad." said Barnett and Alto in unison. Everyone looked at Barnett in surprise. "Yes, my dad!" he growled. "My mom is there too, I can smell her fragrance," Odiferus sighed. Quilla snapped everyone out of their thoughts with a mighty "Let's get this done and get back to the beavers!" The four said "Right!" in unison, and moved to the edge of the lighted area.

"We can move those boxes over against the fence and climb down the other boxes on the other side." Barnett suggested. "Good idea, but those aren't boxes," said Rochelle. They all looked at her. She closed her eyes as she said very slowly, as if recalling a dreadful memory, "They are . . .cages." Each little critter swallowed hard to push the fears aside and gather up some determination.

"How about that tree?" said Odiferus, "The branch hangs over the fence and someone could climb down the . . .cages" They all shuddered and agreed at the same time. Rochelle began to climb, thinking she could open the gate easily enough with her clever paws. Her mother always said, "Rochelle, you have such clever paws." For a baby raccoon, that was like a mom saying you were smart or talented. It made her feel so proud, but now was not the time to dwell on those thoughts. In fact, her thoughts were interrupted by Alto who choked out the word they had heard all night, "wolves."

Barnett and Quilla continued to watch Rochelle climb onto the small branch of the tree, hushing Alto. Again, but a bit louder, he said the word, "wolves." Again, in frustration the two hushed him, telling him to stop playing, as they watched Rochelle move out onto the limb, only to see it sag beneath her weight, landing her back onto the ground with a thump. Rochelle sighed, and caught a familiar, yet stronger, horrific stench. Turning her head, along with Barnett and Quilla, in the direction of the odor, she, along with the others, could only mouth the word stuck deep in their throats, "wolves!"

Sure enough, there they were, a pack of hairy, snarling creatures. Odiferus had quickly turned to face the fence, tail aimed and spraying at the creatures. Quilla's tail was also pointing quills in their direction. Alto's tail was also facing the wolves, but he was mainly trying to dig his way under the fence. Barnett rose on his hind legs and waved his arms as brave bears do, claws pointed. It was at this time Rochelle realized that Barnett was only a cub bear, for he stood, at his tallest, no higher than the back of the smallest wolf, and there were six of them.

CHAPTER X

The wolves paced back and forth; each one had its own special style. There was the leader of the pack, who acted very intelligent. He was handsome in a wolfish sort of way, and strong. He had a twinkle in his eyes that drew you to him and a way of walking that caused you to follow his every move in a spellbound fashion. His mate was just as charming. She had flowing fur, with huge eyes surrounded by eyelashes that fluttered. Her smile was sincere as she leaned in close, only to reveal fangs dripping with desire. The smallest wolf had a big mouth, always trying to impress the leader. He strutted around as if he owned the pack, but all knew otherwise. The other three were awful to look at and of course they, too, were followers-just big troublemakers with scars, which revealed all the fights they had been involved in. They too showed their fangs in a vicious manner, never hiding their intentions.

"Tonight, we will feast on a banquet of young meats, my Lovely." The lead wolf said, nuzzling his mate. The others howled in agreement, and suddenly the forest children each realized the awful mistakes they had made this night. They began screaming for help as loud as they could. Their little bodies moved closer to the fence as the wolves moved closer. The little critters backed even closer to the electric fence, daring not to touch it, and continued to scream for help. Standing their ground, Rochelle yelled, "Dig!" and they all turned in unison and began to dig for their lives.

"My, such a delightful menu." Said the she wolf to her mate. "Whom will we eat first?" asked the leader, baring his fangs and licking his lips. "How about a rat appetizer, boss?" Chuckled one of the pack and with that, it inched itself closer to Alto's tail, giving it a deep sniff.

"Dig, dig, help, help!" screamed Alto, and as hearts pounded and dirt flew, a commotion was heard on the other side of the fence, charging paws, up the piled cages and soaring over the forest children. Another set of four paws passed them overhead.

Soon there was fighting, growls, barks, and howls. The fur was flying on those bad boy wolves. One wolf was wounded and to everyone's surprise Officer Scout and Officer Sarge, the two police dogs from Haven Lake Crisis Center, who Rochelle had met on her very first day, stood over the leader of the pack, snarling only as good police dogs can: "You have the right to remain silent . . ." The words were lost as the sounds of flapping wings were heard overhead. Every one of the forest children looked up towards the moon and saw the shadows of a mass of owls flying above. The wolf was growling, the officers were barking, the pack was howling on the ridge, and the forest children were stunned and crying as Olivia and her army of counselors flew in to scoop up the children. Several were needed for Barnett. All this happened so swiftly, that the three human rangers, who came outside to see what the commotion was all about, only saw their dogs and a wounded wolf to cage.

"What a night!" barked Officer Sarge to Olivia as she flew above the trees. "We'll take care of it from here," she hooted. "We'll get you a report in the morning, Olivia." barked Officer Scout, who was busy growling around the wolf to impress the rangers. They were patting the dogs' heads, telling them what a good job they had done. Rochelle wanted to pat their heads too, but once again, she was being flown away from her mama. This time she was in big trouble and so were the rest of the forest children. The fear was different from the last time Olivia flew her to the crisis center. There was complete silence. No sweet reassuring voice or gentle clutch. Rochelle was firmly held as they maneuvered through the crevice and into the cavern. The others were flown to separate parts of the cavern and placed in other rooms and offices for the night.

Mrs. Opossum was right, just like most grown-up mothers, the center was a big commotion of scurrying around, wings in a flutter, and there sat Mr. and Mrs. Beaver. She was wringing her paws, and he was thumping his tail. Rochelle closed her eyes as she was flown past them. She was too ashamed to make eye contact. She had broken her trust with them. Her mama would be ashamed with her behavior, and what if she had been the wolves' supper. Her mama would be so sad. All of these thoughts welled up in Rochelle, and she curled up in the nest where Olivia placed her. A human doll was placed next to her, but she pushed it away, and remained curled up, facing the wall of stone.

Olivia said nothing, which made matters much worse. Tears flowed freely but Rochelle made no sound. She had done what she had to do, and she did not want anyone to hear her cry, but Olivia knew. Olivia left the bark door ajar so she could make sure Rochelle would be all right for the night. The fireflies worked on shifts, so some of them were leaving for the night. This dimmed the cavern, and soon all the owls were out on a break getting a snack and discussing what to do next with the five forest foster children. Once the owls returned with their snacks, they took Mr. and Mrs. Beaver into an office to discuss what would be done.

Hearing Rochelle's sobs, Barnett lumbered into Olivia's office, finding Rochelle curled up on her nest. She was still awake and her nest was wet with tears. Barnett nudged in beside her and lay down. Soon Odiferus came in and curled up next to Rochelle. Even his odor did not stir anyone. Alto slipped through a hole in the door of his room, scurried across the cavern hidden by roots, and finding no space next to Rochelle, he tiptoed onto Barnett's back and fell asleep. Last, but surprisingly not least, Quilla came into the room and curled near the nest, completely exhausted from the ordeal of the night. They all slept hard and long, feeling like failures and not looking forward to the dawn.

Olivia returned with the Beavers and her intern counselors from their break and serious discussion. One of her counselors hooted that Barnett was missing, and soon each was hooting their discovery of empty nests and nooks. Olivia flew across the cavern with the others behind her, pushing open the bark door to her office. There, in the twilight of the fire-flies, were the five forest foster children sleeping as family, no longer strangers to each other. Olivia smiled and nodded to the other counselors and the Beavers. Their counseling was working, and all were safe this night.

CHAPTER XI

Dawn came too soon for the little critters, and they quickly found themselves facing a very stern-looking owl, other counselors, two police dogs, and Mr. and Mrs. Beaver. The five stood before Olivia as if facing a judge. Her wings were crossed, as were those of the other owls and the beavers' arms. She was shaking her head, and started with a simple, but very complex question. "Well?"

They all began to speak at the same time, sharing the when, where, and why's of the night. It was bedlam, and Olivia unfolded her wings, stretching them out to silence the forest children. She spoke calmly and directly, "You all have had quite an adventure which has given you no results for your mission. You have been dishonest and disobedient to Mr. and Mrs. Beaver. You put your lives in jeopardy several times last night, and also put Police Officers Scout and Sarge in danger. Each of you was told that your parents would soon be with you." Under his breath, Barnett said, "Right, my dad is probably dead!" At the same instant Quilla said softly, "Yes, and I have no parents!" All five straightened up and fearfully glanced up at Olivia and then just as quickly at the ground. "Our job is to keep you safe. You have caused great inconvenience to many others here at the crisis center."

Olivia continued to speak in her calm firm manner; not a feather was ruffled. She was definitely a professional. "In a few days, just as was promised, you are going to be reunited with your families. Until then, Mr. and Mrs. Beaver both want all of you to return to the dam. You must decide now, or we will place you in separate homes until that time. We can have absolutely no more stunts like this from any of you! Is this understood?" She went down the list of names and each forest child understood. "Good." She said with a faint smile, but they didn't see it. Their heads hung in shame most of the way back to the dam. All were caught up in their own thoughts.

Finally, Rochelle broke the silence, as Mr. and Mrs. Beaver led the way with Olivia and the counselors following for good measure. Officer Scout and Officer Sarge were behind the small group heading for Crystal Cove. "Mr. and Mrs. Beaver," Rochelle began. She cleared her throat and stopped. Soon all were surrounding the little raccoon, and the owls were perched in the trees. "I am so sorry for what I caused last night. Please forgive all of us, because Alto, Barnett, Odiferus, and Quilla did this for me. It was my plan, my idea, and my big mistake." Alto jumped into the conversation with, "Now that is just wrong, wrong I say! I wanted to go and see my dad too!" Soon, Barnett was saying he just wanted to see if everyone was telling the truth about his dad, and Odiferus began to quiver as he shared how much he longed for his mother's hug. He cried, but to everyone's surprise, he controlled his scent. Even he looked up in shock, yelling, "I did it! I did it, or more like, I didn't do it! I didn't do it!" A greater surprise was about to be shared, and all stopped cheering Odiferus' new ability to control his urges.

Quilla moved to the center of the circle and softly spoke. "I went with Rochelle, Alto, Odiferus, and Barnett because they are my friends." A hush went over the group and the four rushed to Quilla to give her a group hug. Instantly, the quills were erect and the group quickly backed up. She smiled, "Sorry." She mumbled. Soon everyone was hugging every-one else, and thanking the counselors, the police officers, and the beavers.

CHAPTER XII

At the dam a few days later, everyone was back to their routines with the males helping Mr. Beaver move branches to the never-ending building of the dam. Quilla shadowed Mrs. Beaver to the water's edge, and then would follow her as she moved out of the water. Rochelle gathered little minnows for evening supper for the hungry workers and herself.

Before twilight, Olivia flew into Crystal Cove, landing on a branch. "Good evening Mr. and Mrs. Beaver. I see Barnett is busy working." Mr. Beaver thumped twice for yes, and then whistled, "He sure is a good cub!" "Well, Barnett, a promise is a promise." she said as only Olivia could. Barnett looked up to her and followed her outstretched wing. Over the bluff bounded his father. Barnett took off in such a rush that the branch Alto was helping him carry was dropped right on Alto. Up from the twigs and leaves came a voice saying; "Now that is just wrong! Wrong I say!" and Alto's head popped up to watch the reunion.

"You're alive, Dad! You are alive!" Barnett roared as only a cub bear could. Bear hugs are an awesome thing to see, and hug they did, again and again. Then, much to Barnett's surprise, his mother and baby sister came from the high grasses, with more bear hugs shared.

Barnett was in heaven, and since his dad was able to control his anger, the entire family was reunited. They would live northwest of the dam near Heart River, roaming free, away from humans. This was very close to the beaver dam, so this was good news. They would stay until tomorrow evening and then be on their way. Mr. Bear was more than willing to help knock over some trees for Mr. Beaver. It was a way of saying thank you to Mr. and Mrs. Beaver. Barnett and his dad spoke about anger, his father stressing the importance of using that energy for good, rather than rage. Barnett glowed with pride in his dad, mom, and baby sister. Rochelle smiled, as she watched them from a distance.

After introductions and stories shared, Olivia flew away, and everyone settled down for the night. Barnett slept with his family in a huge hollowed-out redwood. Rochelle said good night to everyone and headed back to the nest she shared with Quilla. The fireflies guided her footsteps, but she heard the soft sobs of Quilla, which led her inside. "Quilla, are you all right?" she asked, feeling dumb about the question as it left her mouth. Of course, she wasn't all right. Everyone had someone coming except Quilla. "I wonder where they will put me next, once all of you are gone?" sobbed Quilla. "Oh, Quilla, Mr. and Mrs. Beaver adore you. You will stay with them." Rochelle softly shared. "But, I am not a beaver, and I can't swim. I will never have a family to hug like the rest." This caused her quills to straighten, and Rochelle and the fireflies dodged the quills by slipping outside. The nest was dark again. Rochelle had big tears swell up in her eyes. There was nothing she could say to comfort Quilla this night. Rochelle slept under the moon and stars, dreaming of her mama.

Early, too early, in the morning a squeaky bellowing voice could be heard all over Crystal Cove, with shouts of, "Now, this is just wrong, wrong I say! Where are you son? Alto where are you?" Sure enough it was Alto's dad, yelling so loud he even woke the frogs that were up all night. Alto sat up straight, hitting his head on a root, and mumbling, "Now, this is just wrong, wrong I say." as he rubbed his forehead, and realized that he wasn't dreaming. His dad was here. He scurried out to see his father maneuvering around the dam's branches. "Dad" Alto screamed as he ran for his father, who was scurrying towards him. Everyone's head was poking out of their resting places to see the two rats embrace. What a celebration rats have as they check out every part of each other between hugs, just to make sure they are each quite well. It was comical and tender at the same time. Alto's dad loudly stated, "No more berries, Alto." Alto gave his dad a strong hug. "No more berries, Dad!" He promised, as he tossed the last one in his paw into the bushes behind his father. Olivia sat on a branch, grinning down at the reunion. Off she flew.

After all met Alto's dad, they listened to his adventures, laughing and enjoying breakfast down by the cove's shore. Quilla stayed at a distance. Both fathers were helping with the logging alongside their sons and

Mr. Beaver. Odiferus was working very hard to keep his mind off his mother and on the task of moving branches. He did not look up as others were talking and laughing. He just concentrated on his job, and then in a moment he recognized a faint familiar fragrance. He ignored it as if it was his imagination, but there it was again. He looked around and nothing stirred. The fragrance was coming from the direction of Firefly Meadow. All of a sudden, through a multitude of wildflowers poked out the tiny head of, of, of - his mother! Odiferus did not care who was nearby, he just let the joy of fragrance race through the air following him as he leaped over small logs and stones making a beeline for his mother. She was alive and not hurt anymore. Their embrace was priceless as only can be imagined between a mother and her son. She cried with joy, and he laughed, talking a mile a minute about his adventure to rescue her, while she held him in her embrace.

Introductions came at a bit of a distance, but all were pleased to meet Mrs. Skunk. Rochelle found her charming and kind, much like Mrs. Beaver. They all laughed and giggled as they shared their stories, and Mrs. Skunk, the bear family, and Mr. Rat shook their heads as they listened to the journey to the Animal Detention Center.

All were apologizing to Mr. and Mrs. Beaver, when all at once Rochelle heard a loud splash. She turned just in time to see Quilla trying to swim near the dam. "Quilla!" She screamed, and all looked in the direction of the dam. Olivia, who had arrived quietly for Odiferus' reunion, flew from one branch to the next and then down to try and grab Quilla. Her quills were erect and straight. "Quilla, lower your quills!" demanded Olivia in her firmest voice ever heard in the forest. Under the water Quilla went, bobbing up and screaming for help.

Her four friends scurried, waddled, and bounded onto the dam, as Quilla was being pulled into the branches. "Help me!" she wailed, coughing water and going under again. "Lower your quills, Quilla!" everyone was shouting. Alto grabbed for her little paw and held it. "Now, this is just wrong, Quilla. Wrong I say." With tears in his eyes, Alto spoke softly. "Please lower your quills. We will save you!" Rochelle cried. Quilla's paw slipped away from Alto, and down she went. Barnett put his paw out to grab her. Odiferus was pulling at branches to keep her from going under the dam. They could tell she was losing her strength. All the parents were trying to get by the children to help, but they were awkward on the dam with the exception of Alto's dad. He got a quill in his paw, and had to move away. All of this was happening in an instant.

Suddenly, Barnett roared louder than ever heard, and in his rage, he demanded that Quilla lower her quills as he leaped into the cove.

"Lower your quills, Quilla, because we love you!" Barnett roared before his head went under the water. In a moment, or perhaps a second, whichever is the quickest; Quilla lowered her quills and sunk beneath the dam. An eternity went by in only a moment, and in an instant Barnett came to the surface holding a wet porcupine in his mouth. He moved out of the water, and Rochelle, Alto, Odiferus and Barnett were hugging the little porcupine, squeezing the water and air out of her. "I'm okay." She gasped, "I'm okay." They continued to hold her until Mr. and Mrs. Beaver approached. Mrs. Beaver hugged her and held her near. "You, my dear, are our little porcupine, and our little beaver. You are our forest child and your home is here." Tears fell from both Mr. and Mrs. Beaver. In fact, there wasn't a dry eye at the cove, including Olivia's, but she flew away to remain professional.

Quilla turned to everyone, hugging them back. It felt so good to be in the arms of so many she trusted, in fact, she would sneak up behind Barnett, Alto and Rochelle to give them a surprise hug. She even gave Odiferus hugs, but never a sneaky one. Wise move on her part.

The beavers had a surprise for Quilla. They had planned to adopt her but had to have a proper room for her in their home. Now, as we all know, beavers have their home inside the dam with only a water entrance available, so it took some time and creativity on the part of Mr. Beaver to get Olivia to okay the new room. Quilla was led through a maze of tunnels, which opened into the Beavers' home. She entered the home through her own bedroom. Once she was in the room, her quills blocked the entrance, and all would be safe. It was ideal, and just for good measure, a bunch of branches swung closed when she would enter the maze. It was perfect! Rochelle and Alto were permitted to see her new home, and Mr. and Mrs. Beaver had a very luxurious home, indeed.

Odiferus and Barnett were waiting as they returned from within the dam. Again it was hugs all around, and Alto, Barnett, and Odiferus said their goodbyes to the new and "improved" Beaverpine family. Quilla giggled as Odiferus came up with the new term. All of them laughed and the five walked to Crystal Cove water's edge to say their goodbyes. Rochelle hugged Barnett, Alto, and Odiferus, not wanting to let them go. "You are the best foster family a raccoon could have." They all smiled, and Barnett hit a tree trunk gently. "Thank you for your friendship and protecting me on our adventure to rescue our folks." They all nodded, trying to be strong forest animal males. They didn't succeed, but Rochelle loved them even more, waving goodbye as they scurried, waddled, and bounded to their parents. Both Quilla and Rochelle put their paws on each other's shoulder and watched, from the bluff overlooking Crystal Cove, to see one by one their friends disappear into the forest or high grasses. Together they sat watching the sun set at Haven Lake.

Just then, Mrs. Beaver called Quilla and Rochelle for supper. "Quilla, I think I'll eat down here tonight." Rochelle sighed, as Quilla gave her another warm hug, and moved off in the direction of the dam and her family. The first fireflies glowed in the high grasses, and just beyond, she could see a familiar silhouette against the sinking sun.

It was Olivia, but she was alone. Olivia landed on the tip of an old log on which Rochelle sat. "Good evening." Olivia gently spoke. "Hi, Olivia" Rochelle sighed. "You have had quite a time, Rochelle, and all in all, I have been very impressed with the way you are growing up." Olivia stated, as her owl head twisted around looking in all directions. "Thank you, Olivia," Rochelle whispered. "You had much influence on your friends, and your mother can be very proud of you, my dear." Olivia replied. Rochelle knew that Olivia, the counselors, and Mr. and Mrs. Beaver truly were the influence, so she was surprised and honored by the words, which were coming from Olivia. "Thank you so much, Olivia!" The little raccoon said. "You are quite welcome, Rochelle." And with that, Olivia flew into the sky aiming for the brightest star, and Haven Lake Crisis Center.

Rochelle was caught off guard at Olivia's sudden exit, but then she heard some noise coming from the high grass, as fireflies winged their way above the green grasses and weeds. She listened, and then shrugged, getting up to head down to the cove.

A small, sweet voice asked, "Would you like some supper, my dear Rochelle?" Rochelle turned and there in the final colors of the evening sun, stood her Mother with a paw filled with minnows. "Mama," the little raccoon cried out, as she scampered to her mother. It felt like she didn't even touch the ground. Suddenly, the small minnows were flopping around on the ground, as her mother dropped them to embrace her daughter. All Rochelle could repeat was "Mama," and that was enough for both of them.

Moments passed, and then her mother looked down into her child's eyes. "Are you hungry?" she asked in her motherly fashion. Rochelle just lovingly gazed up at her mama and nodded, yes. "Well, I think we will dine here at Crystal Cove tonight," her mama said. Both Rochelle and her mama smiled, waddling down to the water's edge together for supper, as the last of the sun slipped into Haven Lake.

Printed in the United States
114447LV00001B